ADVENTURES IN THE INTERNET

Keeping Children Safe Online

JACALYN S. LEAVITT

SALLY SHILL LINFORD

Illustrated by J. Chad Erekson

Foreword by First Lady Laura Bush

WILEY

Wiley Publishing, Inc.

For our children and grandchildren
and every child

Published by John Wiley & Sons, Inc., Indianapolis, Indiana
Published simultaneously in Canada

The character Faux Paw; the names "Faux Paw," "Faux Paw the Techno Cat," "the Techno Cat," "iKeepSafe," "3 Keeps," and "Internet Keep Safe Coalition"; the stylized six-toed paw print; and the slogan "Keep Safe • Keep Away • Keep Telling" are legally protected service marks and trademarks of the Internet Keep Safe Coalition.

For general information about our other products and services, please contact our Customer Care Department within the United States at (800) 762-2974, outside the United States at (317) 572-3993 or fax (317) 572-4002.

Wiley also publishes its books in a variety of electronic formats. Some content that appears in print may not be available in electronic books. For more information about Wiley products, visit our web site at www.wiley.com.

ISBN-13: 978-0-470-05137-5
ISBN-10: 0-470-05137-X

Printed in the United States of America

10 9 8 7 6 5 4 3 2 1

FOREWORD

THE WHITE HOUSE

Dear Parents,

Recent news stories have made us all aware how sexual predators use the Internet to entrap and victimize children. As part of President Bush's *Helping America's Youth* initiative, we want to reinforce to parents, educators, youth leaders, and law enforcement officials that you don't have to be a computer expert to protect a child from this growing threat. If children learn early to safeguard their personal information and to keep far away from Internet strangers, they will not become victims of this frightening epidemic.

As community members, we can and must work together to ensure that all children receive this urgent message. I encourage all adults to teach children the basic principles of online safety that are found in this book. Thank you for your commitment to our shared priority of protecting children everywhere.

Sincerely,

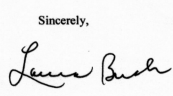

Hello, I'm Faux Paw the Techno Cat.

I used to live in the animal shelter, but not anymore. The governor rescued me. Now the state capitol building is my home.

I live in the governor's office, where I'm an important part of the team. There's a big ball of yarn that I'm in charge of. And when the governor's had a tough day, I sit at his feet. I can tell he feels better.

You say my name "foe-paw." In France, *faux pas* means mistake or false step, but I'm named Faux Paw because I have an extra toe on each of my front paws. (Get it?)

Everybody makes *faux pas* sometimes, but let me tell you about a really big mistake I made.

It happened on the computer. Most people don't put cats and computers together, but I'm the Techno Cat for a good reason. I'm a computer whiz! At night, when everyone goes home, the governor lets me use his laptop. I am soooo good at games.

One night I was cruising around Internet City using my favorite part of the computer—the mouse! LOL. (On the Internet, that means "laugh out loud." Sometimes I even make myself LOL.)

    While I was mousing around, I bumped into the governor's old friend, Cursor. He and the governor work together all the time.

    "Howdy, Faux Paw," he said. "Don't forget—the Internet is like a big city. Some places are safe, other places aren't, and it's important to know the difference."

But how could I listen to Cursor? Right before my eyes was the Ball-of-Yarn Chat Room—a dream come true! Flashing signs, piles of yarn, free catnip giveaways! And . . .

. . . a new friend: Happy Fluffy Kittyface! Words just showed up on my screen.

"**Hello, Faux Paw,**" she typed, "**I'm Happy Fluffy Kittyface. Wanna chat?**"

So I typed back: "**Oh, Kittyface, I haven't had anyone to talk to all day. Everyone's so busy here.**"

"That's okay," she typed, "I'd love to be your Internet friend. I like to purr in the sunshine and play with yarn, how about you?"

"THAT'S MY FAVORITE THING IN ALL THE WORLD!" I shouted back.

"Faux Paw," she asked, "maybe we go to the same school? Do you go to Meow-Meow Elementary?"

I was just about to tell her that I go to Cool Cats Elementary, but Cursor jumped in: "No, Faux Paw! Never tell anyone on the Internet the name of your school!"

"Silly Cursor," I thought, "he loves to say things like that—he's such a worrier."

Luckily, Kittyface was still there. She typed, **"Faux Paw, I have a new ball of yarn—bright red—wanna see it?"**

"Oh, yes! I'd love to see your ball of yarn," I typed.

"Let's play," she typed. **"I'll bring my yarn, and you bring yours. Maybe we can watch a movie. Where do you live?"**

Cursor was going crazy by now. "No, Faux Paw!" he said. "Never give your name, address, phone number, the name of your school, or even a picture of yourself to anyone on the Internet."

I thought, "Cursor just doesn't understand—Happy Fluffy Kittyface is my friend." So I kept typing: **"Let's meet by the lamppost in front of the capitol building."**

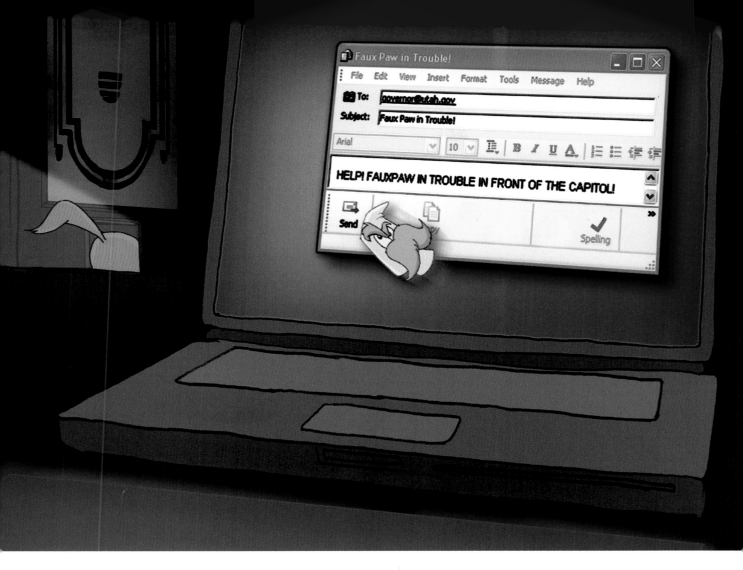

"Stop, Faux Paw! Never, *never* meet anyone you've found in a chat room!"

But I thought I knew better than silly Cursor. "Sorry, Cursor, got to go. I have a new best friend to meet," I said.

"Faux Paw! I'm worried! I'd better alert the governor!" he said as I ran out the door.

When I got to the lamppost, it was a lot darker than I thought it would be. "Where's Happy Fluffy Kittyface?" I thought.

"I can't wait to show her my official pillow by the governor's desk and the candy machines in the basement. I wonder if her ball of yarn is bigger than mine.

"... She sure is taking her time."

Then a voice came from behind me. It wasn't a happy, fluffy voice.

It was a low, terrible growl. "Hullo, Faux Paw, I'm Happy Fluffy . . .

"...Kittyface!"

I ran as fast as my four legs and twenty-two toes would carry me, but it wasn't fast enough!

"Where can I hide? Somebody, help! Cursor!" I screamed.

Just when I thought I was doomed, the governor's car screeched around the corner. He threw open the door and yelled, "Hurry, Faux Paw!"

I jumped straight into the arms of the governor, someone I knew I could trust.

"Wow, am I glad to see you!" I said. "Kittyface almost ate me alive."

"You were lucky tonight, Faux Paw," said the governor. "You've got a good friend in Cursor."

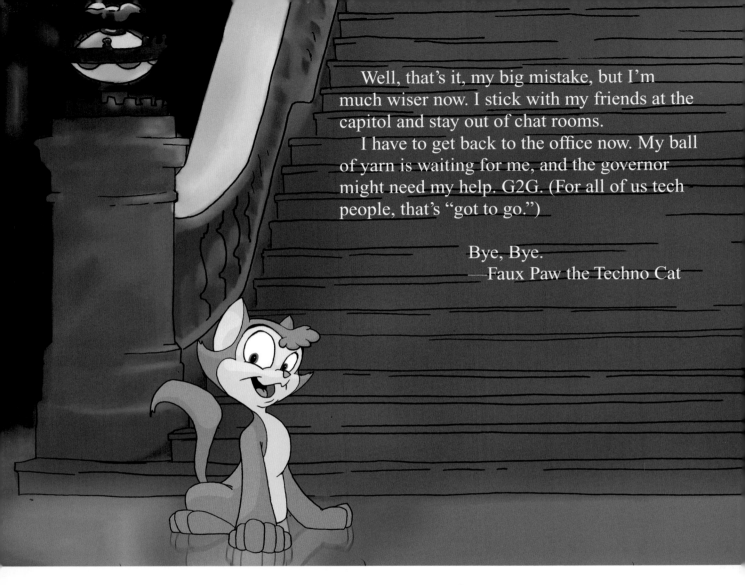

Well, that's it, my big mistake, but I'm much wiser now. I stick with my friends at the capitol and stay out of chat rooms.

I have to get back to the office now. My ball of yarn is waiting for me, and the governor might need my help. G2G. (For all of us tech people, that's "got to go.")

Bye, Bye.
—Faux Paw the Techno Cat

The End

But keep going . . .

Howdy, kids! I'm your friend Cursor. Remember, the Internet is like a big city with great places to go, but you have to be careful.

That's why we have the **3 KEEPs**™ of Internet safety:

Keep Safe • Keep Away • Keep Telling™

I keep safe my personal information—all of it! I never give my real name, address, phone number, the name of my school, or a picture of myself to anyone online.

I keep away from Internet strangers—no matter what they tell me, because I have no way of knowing who they really are. I don't talk with them online, and I never meet them face-to-face.

I keep telling my parents or a trusted adult about everything I see on the Internet—especially when something makes me uncomfortable.

. . . So long, friends.

If you want to read more about Faux Paw the Techno Cat and Internet safety, check out the iKeepSafe Web site:

www.iKeepSafe.org

www.iKeepSafe.org

Brought To You By

 AOL

 symantec™

 Adobe

 *BearingPoint*

 CONVERGYS
Out*thinking* Out*doing*

DELL™

 Disney Online

 (intel)

SIEBEL.

RONALD MCDONALD
HOUSE CHARITIES

 TARGET

 WASATCH

THE J. WILLARD AND ALICE S.
MARRIOTT FOUNDATION

Associations and Specialists:

American Academy of Pediatrics • American Medical Association • American Medical Association Alliances
Cable in the Classroom • Childhelp • D.A.R.E. America • Enough Is Enough
GetNetWise.org • InfraGard • National Association of Broadcasters
National Crime Prevention Council, McGruff the Crime Dog • National Education Association
National PTA • The National Cable and Telecommunications Association
Newspaper Association of America • Optimist International • Web Wise KidsWired Safety
Wired Kids • Parry Aftab, Internet Attorney
Michael Rich, MD, Director of the Center on Media and Child Health, Harvard University

Parents,

You don't have to be a computer expert to keep your child safe online. The Parent Resource Center at www.iKeepSafe.org is specifically designed to help you help your child navigate the Web safely. There you'll find:

- **Parents' top 10 Internet safety questions—answered!**
- **Video library with quick and easy information on critical safety issues**
- **Family Fun Lessons for teaching children how to keep safe online**
- **D.A.R.E. Activity Center with Internet safety activities for children**

- **Online moderated discussion group for parents**
- **Instructions for how to report Internet crimes**
- **Internet legal questions answered**
- **Instruction by topic that will keep you current with kids' technology use**

Keep current by signing up to receive ongoing updates and product tutorials as they're released.

Parents — you'll find Faux Paw's books at your favorite bookseller. Teachers, librarians, and community leaders — please contact specialsales@wiley.com to find out how you can use the Faux Paw books to teach Internet safety.